The Boxcar Children Mysteries

THE GREAT DETECTIVE RACE

created by
GERTRUDE CHANDLER WARNER

Illustrated by Robert Papp

ALBERT WHITMAN & Company
Albert Whitman & Company

The Great Detective Race
Created by Gertrude Chandler Warner;
Illustrated by Robert Papp.

ISBN: 978-0-8075-5573-6 (hardcover)
ISBN: 978-0-8075-5574-3 (paperback)

Cover art by Robert Papp.

For information about Albert Whitman & Company,
visit our web site at www.albertwhitman.com.

Contents

THE GREAT DETECTIVE RACE

CHAPTER 1

Ready . . . Set . . . Go!

"It just hit me!" cried six-year-old Benny. He snapped his fingers. "I know the perfect gift!"

Ten-year-old Violet looked over at her little brother. "What's that, Benny?" she asked.

"A book about codes and clues!"

"Oh, Benny!" Jessie, who was twelve, couldn't help laughing. "That's a perfect gift for *us.* "

"We're supposed to be looking for something for Mrs. McGregor," Henry pointed out.

Henry was fourteen. He was the oldest of the Aldens.

"Not everybody likes mysteries as much as we do, Benny," Violet said. In fact, the Aldens loved mysteries. And together, they'd managed to solve quite a few.

"Mrs. McGregor loves cooking," Jessie reminded Benny.

The four Alden children—Henry, Jessie, Violet, and Benny—were standing in the Rat Cellar, a bookstore in Greenfield. They were shopping for a birthday present for their housekeeper.

"Yes," said Benny. "Mrs. McGregor's the best cook in the whole world."

"Yes," Jessie said thoughtfully. "Maybe we should be looking at cookbooks."

"That's a great idea," agreed Henry. Benny nodded.

But Violet wasn't so sure. "Mrs. McGregor already has so many cookbooks. Don't you think we should get her something really special, Jessie?"

Jessie wasn't listening. Something had caught

her eye. The others followed her gaze to a poster on the wall.

"The ballet's performing *Swan Lake* at the Greenfield Theater," Jessie said. "And Mrs. McGregor loves ballet!"

"Oh, Jessie!" Violet clapped her hands. "That really *would* be the perfect gift!"

There was no stopping Benny. The youngest Alden raced over to the checkout. "We'd like to buy a ticket to *Swan Lake*, please," he told the salesclerk.

The other Aldens smiled. They could always count on Benny to act fast.

The young woman behind the counter shook her head. "I'm afraid we don't sell them here. Why don't you try the ticket outlet in the Greenfield Mall," she suggested.

"Thanks," said Henry. "We will."

As they turned to go, a smartly dressed woman, her hair streaked with gray, suddenly stormed through the door.

"Not a single copy!" she almost shouted. "I don't see a single copy of *The Art of Good Manners* in sight." The woman glared at the salesclerk. "You promised to display my books in your store window."

"Oh!" The young woman behind the counter blinked in surprise. "You must be the author—Amber Madison."

"Well, who else would I be? I came all the way from Boston to promote my book. But it looks like I made the trip for nothing!"

"I'm so sorry, Miss Madison," the salesclerk apologized. "We've been rather busy around—"

"I'm not interested in your excuses!" the author snapped, cutting her short. "Do your job—or else!" With that, Amber Madison walked out.

The salesclerk let out a sigh as the door closed. "You'll have to excuse me," she told the Aldens. "I have work to do."

"No problem," said Henry. "Thanks for your help."

As they stepped outside, Jessie shook her head. "I think Amber Madison should read her own book on manners."

Benny frowned. "She wasn't very nice."

"I guess she was disappointed," said Violet, who always liked to think the best of people. "About her books, I mean."

"That doesn't excuse her for being rude," Jessie insisted, as they headed for the mall.

"One thing's for sure," put in Henry, "a book on manners is the very last thing Mrs. McGregor needs."

"Mrs. McGregor's *always* polite," agreed Benny.

"We're lucky to have her in our lives," Violet said with a nod.

After their parents died, the four Alden children had run away. For a while, their home was an empty boxcar in the woods. But then their grandfather, James Alden, found them, and he brought them to live with him in his big white house in Connecticut. Even the boxcar was given a special place in the backyard. The children often used it as a clubhouse.

Inside the mall, the Aldens headed straight for the ticket outlet. "Mrs. McGregor will be so surprised," Violet said, her eyes dancing.

Jessie put the money on the counter. "We'd like a ticket to *Swan Lake*, please."

"Sorry." The tall man behind the ticket window shook his head. "I just sold the last one."

The Aldens could hardly believe their ears. "Now what?" Benny asked, his shoulders slumped.

Henry glanced at his watch. "It's almost lunch time," he said. "Why don't we stop for a bite to eat."

Benny didn't need to be asked twice. The youngest Alden was known for his appetite. In no time at all, the four children were carrying their trays to an empty table in the food court. Violet and Jessie were sharing a ham and cheese submarine sandwich. Henry had chosen fish and chips. And Benny's plate was piled high with fried chicken, cole slaw, and potato salad. While music blasted from the overhead speakers, the Aldens turned their attention back to Mrs. McGregor's birthday gift.

"I guess we could still get a cookbook," said Henry.

Benny nodded. "Maybe one with cookie recipes in it."

"Sounds more like a present for *you*, Benny," Henry teased.

Benny grinned. "Well, I *do* like—" The youngest Alden suddenly stopped talking.

"What is it, Benny?" Jessie asked with a worried frown. She often acted like a mother to her younger brother and sister.

Benny put a finger to his lips. "Shh, listen!"

No one spoke for a moment. They heard a man's voice coming from the radio on the overhead speakers.

"You heard me, folks! Free tickets to Swan Lake! But remember, time's running out to sign up for the Great Detective Race. This week, radio station WGFD is coming to you on location in the Greenfield Mall. Just head for our booth—right behind Alice—and fill out an entry form. Track down the right code word and win front-row seats to Swan Lake—as well as a ride in the sky with our very own traffic reporter, Chopper Dan. I'll be interviewing the winner on my afternoon program, so sign up now. Just tell them Mike Devlin sent you!"

Violet's hand flew to her mouth in surprise. "Did he just say something about free tickets to *Swan Lake?*"

Jessie nodded. "Front-row seats for the winner of the Great Detective Race!"

"And we're detectives!" cried Benny, his eyes shining. "We'll win for sure, right, Henry?"

"Right!" Henry agreed. Then he added honestly, "At least, we'll do our best."

The four Aldens quickly finished their lunch. Then they hurried over to a fountain decorated with a statue of a mermaid.

The stone mermaid, nicknamed Alice, was holding a mirror and smiling to herself. People in Greenfield often made a wish as they threw coins into the water. The bottom of the fountain was covered in pennies, dimes, and nickels. All the money went to charity.

Benny looked at his brother. Henry knew why. "Here you go, Benny," he said, fishing a penny from his pocket.

With a grin, Benny took the penny and tossed it into the water.

"I bet that's Mike Devlin," Henry said, nodding in the direction of a booth nearby.

The other Aldens looked over to see a young man of about thirty sitting behind a microphone. He had sandy-colored hair and a golden tan.

"I'm sure of it," said Jessie. She pointed to a WGFD poster with photos of both Mike Devlin and "Chopper Dan" Beamer.

Henry, Jessie, Violet, and Benny hurried over where a crowd had gathered around a long table. Everyone was busy filling out entry forms.

"Hi, kids!" A smiling young woman with coppery-red hair greeted the Aldens. "Are you here to sign up for the Great Detective Race?"

The youngest Alden nodded. "I'm Benny. And this is my brother Henry, and my sisters, Jessie and Violet."

"Nice to meet you. I'm Debra Belmont."

"It's nice to meet you, too," said Jessie, speaking for them all.

"It's my job to get more people to listen to this station," Debra explained. "The more

listeners, the better." She handed each of the children a WGFD baseball cap.

"Cool!" said Henry.

"Just fill out an entry form," Debra went on. "Then I'll give you the first clue. All the other clues are hidden somewhere in town. Oh, by the way," she added, "you might need to use the magic words—'I listen to the Big G.'"

"How dare you stick me on your Late Night show!" A woman stepped up to the table, waving a letter in the air. "I was expecting an interview with Mike Devlin."

The Aldens looked at each other in surprise. It was Amber Madison—the author of *The Art of Good Manners.*

"I'm afraid that's not possible, Miss Madison," Debra explained, as nicely as possible. "We never do interviews during the daytime."

"Oh?" Amber looked cross. "Won't Mike Devlin be interviewing the winner of this . . . this silly race on his program?"

"Yes, but it's just for the contest," Debra told her.

"I'm promoting my book!" Amber argued.

"Nobody listens to the radio late at night. I want to talk about my book during the *day*."

"I'm sorry, but it just can't be done," Debra said with a shrug. "We do interviews at night."

"I see." Amber looked as if she wanted to argue, but she didn't. Instead, she sat down on the edge of the fountain, shaking her head.

Benny's eyes were round. "That lady sure gets upset a lot."

"Some grown-ups are like that," said Henry, putting an arm around his brother.

On the other side of the table, a boy about Henry's age suddenly called out, "Does spelling count?"

Debra shook her head. "Don't worry," she said with a smile. "I'm not much of a speller myself. If you can figure out clues, that's all that matters in this race."

"Guess what?" Benny piped up, as Jessie filled out an entry form. "We like tracking down clues—and we're good at it, too!"

"Oh, really?" Debra looked over in surprise.

"We *have* solved quite a few mysteries," Henry admitted.

"Well, good luck with this one," Debra said, holding out an envelope. "The first clue's a real doozy!"

As the Aldens walked away, they didn't notice the boy on the other side of the table frowning—or Amber Madison watching them carefully.

CHAPTER 2

The Pied Piper

"We were in the mall," Benny was telling Grandfather at dinner that night, "and guess what we heard on the overhead speakers?"

"I have a hunch it had something to do with a mystery," answered Grandfather. "Am I right?"

Benny's jaw dropped. "How did you know?"

Grandfather chuckled. "Because my grandchildren have a way of attracting mysteries."

"The Greenfield radio station is having

a contest, Grandfather," Henry said. "The Great Detective Race."

Jessie added, "There's a code word hidden somewhere in town. The first person who finds it, wins the race."

"We're hoping to win tickets to *Swan Lake*," Violet said. She looked to make sure their housekeeper wasn't around. "For Mrs. McGregor's birthday," she whispered behind her hand.

Grandfather nodded approvingly. "That's a great idea."

"And that's not all," Benny added. "The winner gets a ride with Chopper Dan—in his helicopter!"

"Well, it's not Chopper Dan's helicopter, Benny," Henry corrected. "I'm pretty sure it belongs to the radio station."

"It won't be an easy race to win," Jessie said. "Lots of people were signing up for the contest."

"Unless I miss my guess," Grandfather said, pushing back his chair, "my grandchildren will have this mystery wrapped up in no time."

The Aldens got up to clear the table as their grandfather left the room.

"Debra was right," Henry said, stacking the dinner plates. "That first clue really *is* a doozy!"

"Why don't you read it again, Henry," Violet suggested, as they carried the dishes into the kitchen.

Henry read the riddle aloud:

The Pied Piper's tune
is the sweetest of all;
to find the next clue,
just answer his call.

"I remember that story," Benny said, handing Jessie an empty platter. "The Pied Piper saved a town from rats."

Jessie nodded as she opened up the dishwasher. "He saved the town of Hamelin."

"But Hamelin wouldn't pay the piper's fee," added Henry, "so he decided to teach them a lesson."

"What did he do again?" Benny wanted to know.

"He played a tune on his pipe," Violet

reminded him. "All the children followed him out of town."

Benny frowned. "Did that really happen?"

"No, it's just a story, Benny," Jessie told him.

"Then how can we follow his call?" Benny wanted to know. "If he isn't real, I mean."

"Good question," Henry said. He gathered the dirty forks and knives and put them into the dishwasher rack.

Just then, Mrs. McGregor came into the room. "I never imagined they'd be sold out already," she said, more to herself than anyone else.

"Is anything wrong, Mrs. McGregor?" Violet asked.

"I was hoping to get tickets to see the ballet, Violet," Mrs. McGregor told her. "But it looks like I'm out of luck." She reached her sewing basket down from the cupboard with a sigh. "I guess the early bird gets the worm."

As their housekeeper left the room, Violet shook her head. "Mrs. McGregor looked so disappointed. I sure hope we can win those tickets for her."

Henry nodded. "The answer's got to be somewhere in the story of the Pied Piper of Hamelin."

"There's something about that name that rings a bell," said Jessie.

"What name, Jessie?" Benny wondered. "The Pied Piper?"

Jessie shook her head. "No, not that," she said. "I'm talking about the name of the town. I have a feeling—" Her face suddenly lit up, then she dashed from the room.

A moment later, Jessie came back waving a street map in the air. "I want to check something out," she told them.

The other Aldens gathered round while Jessie opened the map. As she bent over the table to look at it, she suddenly thumped her finger down. "I knew it sounded familiar!" she said, pointing to a street just behind the Greenfield tennis courts.

Henry, Violet, and Benny took a closer look. "It's Hamelin Lane!" Violet realized.

"That's good detective work, Jessie!" said Henry. He slapped his sister a high-five. So did Violet and Benny.

"You think that's where we'll find the next clue?" asked Benny. "Somewhere on Hamelin Lane?"

"That'd be my guess," said Jessie.

Benny let out a cheer. It was always fun figuring out clues.

*   *   *

After breakfast the next morning, the Aldens put on their WGFD baseball caps and hopped on their bikes. With Watch beside them, they set off for Hamelin Lane. Henry held their little dog's leash as they pedaled along. They were careful not to go too fast so that Watch could keep up with them.

"Keep your eyes peeled," Henry advised when they reached the lane behind the tennis courts. "Remember, anything unusual can be a clue."

The children rode up and down Hamelin Lane. Once ... twice ... three times.

They saw a teenager cutting the grass, kids throwing a Frisbee, and a woman knitting at her kitchen window. But they saw nothing that would help them win the Great Detective Race. They finally stopped.

"I was so sure we were on the right track," Jessie said, as they walked their bikes across the grassy lawn by the tennis courts.

Henry nodded. "The clues seemed to fit." Benny had a thought. "Maybe we should be looking for rats."

"Ooooh!" Violet shivered. "Do you really think so, Benny?"

"Well, The Pied Piper of Hamelin *was* a story about rats."

"You might be on to something, Benny," Henry said thoughtfully.

Jessie turned to her older brother. "What are you thinking, Henry?"

"What's the name of the bookstore?" Henry asked.

Jessie snapped her fingers as she remembered. "The Rat Cellar!"

Benny grinned. "Now we're getting somewhere."

With that, they headed down Main Street. While Violet waited on the sidewalk with Watch, the other Aldens went inside the Rat Cellar to look for clues. They searched up one aisle and down another. They even checked out the books on the bargain table. But it was no use.

"Looks like we struck out again," Henry said, heading for the door.

"Wait a minute, Henry." Benny pulled on his brother's arm. "We're forgetting something."

Henry turned around. "What's that, Benny?"

"Remember what Debra Belmont said?" he reminded them. "About the magic words, I mean."

"Oh, right!" said Henry. "Good thinking."

With that, Benny walked up to the salesclerk. "I listen to the Big G!" he announced.

"What . . . ?" The salesclerk looked startled. "That's, um, . . . nice," she said, then hurried away to help a customer.

"Well, that didn't work," Henry said as they stepped outside.

"No luck?" Violet asked.

Jessie shook her head. "Zero."

Violet had been thinking. "There's a music store just down the street. Let's check it out."

"A music store?" Henry looked puzzled, but only for a moment. "Oh, because the Pied Piper played music on his pipe, right?"

"Exactly," said Violet, taking her bike from the rack.

"Hi there, kids!" said a voice behind them.

As they whirled around, Amber Madison flashed them a smile. The children were so surprised by the author's friendly greeting, they were speechless for a moment.

"You're the Aldens, right?" Amber went on. "I noticed you signing up for the Great Detective Race. Are you getting anywhere with it?"

"Not really," said Jessie. "Not yet, anyway."

"Oh," said Amber. "Too bad." She sounded disappointed.

"But we're getting warmer," Benny said.

Amber lifted an eyebrow. "Oh?" She flashed

them another smile. "I'd love to hear all about it," she said. "I find it quite fascinating."

Jessie suddenly felt very uncomfortable. "We have to go," she said, glancing at her watch. "Sorry."

The Aldens hurried away.

"That was weird," Jessie said, when they were out of earshot. "How did Amber Madison know who we were?"

"We didn't tell her our names," said Benny.

"Maybe she overheard us talking at the mall," suggested Violet. "I noticed her sitting on the edge of the fountain nearby."

But Jessie wondered if Amber Madison had asked someone who they were. But why?

When they got to the music store, they soon forgot all about the author. Jessie, Violet, and Benny gave the shop a careful search while Henry had waited outside with Watch. They checked out the flute section twice. They even said the magic words to the salesclerk. But he just looked puzzled. Finally, they stepped outside again, shaking their heads.

"Another dead end?" Henry asked.

Violet nodded. "Looks that way."

Just then, Benny caught his breath. "Look!"

The others followed their little brother's gaze down the street. "Oh my gosh!" cried Violet. "Is that what I think it is?"

Jessie nodded. "It's a . . . a giant turkey!"

Henry laughed. "I think it's just Dennis Howe in some kind of turkey getup!" Dennis was a college student—and one of the Aldens' neighbors.

Sure enough, Dennis greeted them with a cheery smile. "Good to see you again, kids!"

"Cool costume!" chirped Benny.

"Actually, it's anything *but* cool, Benny," Dennis said, as he knelt down to pet Watch. "I'm roasting under all these feathers."

"So . . . why are you dressed up like a turkey, Dennis?" Henry wanted to know.

"Goes with the job." Dennis looked up as he scratched Watch behind the ears. "I'm handing out fliers for the Turkey Trot dance studio," he explained. "And what are you kids doing in town?"

"We're on the hunt for clues," Jessie told him. "We're taking part in the Great Detective Race."

"That explains the baseball caps," Dennis said, standing up. "They're very popular around here lately."

The Aldens glanced around at the shoppers. Dennis was right. Half the people in town seemed to be wearing WGFD baseball caps! Could they find the code word before anyone else?

CHAPTER 3

Three Strikes in a Row

After dinner, the children took turns telling Grandfather about their day as they relaxed on the front porch. Watch was dozing nearby while the evening shadows grew longer. Benny finished by saying, "We kept striking out."

James Alden smiled over at his younger grandson. "I have a hunch there's a clue just around the next corner, Benny," he said. "Speaking of WGFD," he added, "here comes Jordan Porter." Grandfather waved as a man in shorts and a white T-shirt came jogging by. Waving back, the silver-haired man turned into the walkway and ran up the porch steps. Grandfather introduced the children to Mr. Porter, the owner of the WGFD radio station.

"Guess what?" Benny said as he shook hands. "We just signed up for the Great Detective Race!"

Jessie nodded. "We've been looking for clues all day."

Mr. Porter nodded approvingly. "We're hoping to drum up more listeners with the race," he explained. "The station just hired someone new. The race was her idea."

"Debra Belmont," guessed Violet. "Right?"

"Right!" Mr Porter said. "So far, she's been doing a great job. But I must admit, she hasn't had an easy time of it."

Grandfather raised an eyebrow. "Oh?"

"Mike Devlin can be a bit difficult sometimes," said Mr. Porter. "He's a good deejay. But I'm afraid he thinks he's too important. He seems to forget it takes teamwork to make a successful radio station."

"Or solve a mystery!" said Benny.

Mr. Porter smiled at the youngest Alden.

"You'll get no argument from me, Benny." With that, the station owner gave them a friendly wave and hurried away.

"Well, I still have paperwork to finish," Grandfather said, getting to his feet. "Sounds like you have your work cut out for you, too," he added. "So I'll leave you to your detective business."

As the screen door closed, Jessie fished the riddle from her pocket and glanced at it again. "There must be something here we're not getting," she said.

Just then, Watch let out a whine. He tilted his head as if he were listening to something that no one else could hear. A moment later, an ice cream truck came around the corner, a happy tune coming from its speakers.

"Do we have enough money for ice cream, Henry?" Benny wanted to know.

Henry took out his money and counted the change. "You're in luck, Benny. Looks like we have enough."

The four Aldens were soon racing down the street with Watch close behind. When the truck slowed to a stop, they joined a long line of children waiting for ice cream.

Violet had a sudden thought. "The ice-cream man is a bit like the Pied Piper," she noted. "Don't you think?"

Henry turned to look at her. "What do you mean?"

"Well, he plays a tune and all the kids follow him down the street," Violet explained. Then she caught her breath, surprised by her own words. "Oh my gosh!" she cried. *"The Pied Piper's tune is the sweetest of all!"*

"And ice cream is sweet!" Benny exclaimed, catching on.

"I think you just found the Pied Piper, Violet!" Jessie said.

Henry added, "Now let's see if the magic words work on him."

When they got to the front of the line, Benny piped up, "We listen to the Big G!"

The young man handing out ice cream suddenly smiled. Then he reached into his pocket and pulled out a WGFD envelope. The Aldens raced home with ice cream bars *and* the next clue.

"Read it, Jessie," Benny urged, inching his porch chair closer. He couldn't read very well yet.

"Here goes," said Jessie, tucking her long hair behind her ears. She read aloud:

Make your way to an alley,
that's what you should do.
Three strikes in a row
and you'll find the next clue.

Benny looked confused. "We already struck out three times."

This made Jessie smile a little. "That's true, Benny," she said. "But I think this means something else."

Violet giggled. "Grandfather was right."

Henry looked over at her. "Right about what, Violet?"

"He said there was a clue coming around the next corner," she reminded them. "And there was!"

Benny nodded. "The Pied Piper came

around the corner driving his ice-cream truck."

"Grandfather was right about something else, too," Henry said thoughtfully. "We've really got our work cut out for us."

Violet nodded. "Greenfield has dozens of back alleys."

"Let's take another look at the map," Jessie said.

In no time at all, the Aldens were huddled around the street map again. Jessie put a red check mark beside every alleyway.

"Whew!" Benny licked a drop of chocolate ice cream from the back of his hand. "This'll take forever."

Violet agreed. "Looks like we have a lot of ground to cover. Any idea where we should begin?"

"I'm not sure," Jessie answered, without taking her gaze off the map.

Henry smiled. "I think we can narrow it down a little," he said. "I have a feeling we should start right here." He placed a finger on the map.

Jessie looked from her older brother to the map and back again. "Behind the ballpark?" she said. "Why do you say that, Henry?"

"I know!" said Benny. *"Three strikes in a row. That means baseball!"*

Henry nodded. "Exactly."

CHAPTER 4

Gobble, Gobble

"Sorry, Watch," Benny said the next morning. "You can't come with us this time." He knelt down and gave their little dog a hug. "We might be gone all day."

Henry petted Watch softly on the head. "We'll take you for a walk after dinner, Watch," he promised.

A few minutes later, the Aldens were riding towards the ballpark. It was a perfect day for a race—the sky was clear and the sun was shining.

The four children rode up and down the narrow alleyway behind the ballpark. They searched carefully for a clue. But after a while, they stopped and looked at one another in dismay.

"Well, I guess I was wrong," Henry said. "And you know what that means."

Jessie glanced over at him. "What?"

"We'll have to search every alley in Greenfield," Henry said.

No one said anything as they pedaled along. There was nothing to say. What could they do except check all over town? They couldn't think of any other way to find the next clue.

All morning long, they rode their bikes up one alley and down another. Finally, Benny had a suggestion. "Maybe we should check the alley behind the diner," he said, as they stopped to wait for a light to change. The youngest Alden wiggled his eyebrows, making everyone laugh.

"We get the hint, Benny," said Henry. "Let's get something to eat."

It wasn't long before they were settled into a booth at the diner. They each ordered the special—chicken burgers, salad, and lemonade. While they waited for their food to arrive, they talked about the race.

"I was so sure the riddle was leading us to the alley behind the ballpark," said Henry.

"The clues added up," Violet said with a nod.

"Wait a minute!" Henry suddenly had an idea that hadn't occurred to him before. "I just thought of a sport with strikes in it."

"We already figured that out, Henry," Benny reminded him. "It's baseball."

Henry shook his head. "I think we got the wrong sport."

"But, Henry," Benny argued, "there are strikes in baseball."

"Yes," Henry agreed, "but there's another sport with strikes in it, too. Come to think of it . . . " He paused to sort out his thoughts. "It's a sport you play in an alley!"

"I'm not following, Henry," said Jessie.

Violet looked just as puzzled as her sister.

"A sport with strikes . . . that you play in an alley?"

"Oh!" said Jessie. "Bowling!"

"Oh, right!" Benny's face lit up. "If you knock down all the bowling pins, it's called a strike."

"And the Greenfield Bowling Alley is just around the corner," Violet said.

"We'll check it out right after lunch," said Jessie. She was handing everyone a napkin from the dispenser when something caught her eye. "Isn't that Debra Belmont over there?"

Henry nodded. "And that's Mike Devlin sitting across from her."

The children didn't mean to eavesdrop. But from where they were sitting, they couldn't help hearing what the two people were talking about.

"But Mike," Debra was saying, "when I first told you about the Great Detective Race, you said it was a cool idea."

"Well, now I'm not so sure." Mike did not sound very happy. "Why are so many kids signing up for this race? Will you please tell me that?"

"It's summer vacation, Mike. I wanted the race to appeal to kids. They listen to our station, too."

"Kids don't listen to *my* show. My listeners are between the ages of twenty and fifty!" Mike was talking loudly now. "Or have you forgotten?"

"No, but . . . "

"No buts about it, Debra." Mike got to his feet. "You just make sure the winner isn't some kid!" With that, he stormed out of the diner.

As Debra hurried after the deejay, Violet turned to her sister and brothers. "I wonder what that was all about?" she whispered.

"Mike Devlin really *can* be difficult," said Jessie, recalling Mr. Porter's words.

Benny swallowed a bite of his burger. "I don't think Mike likes kids."

"Well, one thing's for sure," said Henry. "Mike doesn't want anyone under the age of twenty to win the race."

"It doesn't make sense," said Violet. "How can Debra make sure a kid doesn't find the code word?"

Jessie took a sip of lemonade. "Let's concentrate on one mystery at a time," she suggested.

That did seem like a good idea. "The important thing right now," said Henry, "is to find the code word."

After finishing their lunch, the Aldens headed over to the Greenfield Bowling Alley. As they rounded the corner, Jessie looked back over her shoulder. Was somebody following them?

"What is it, Jessie?" Henry asked.

"I'm not sure," said Jessie, keeping her voice low. She didn't want to frighten Violet and Benny. "I just feel like somebody's watching us."

Henry looked behind them. But he didn't see anybody.

"There's nobody there now, Jessie," he assured her.

"I'm probably just imagining things,"

Jessie said, trying to make light of it. But something didn't seem right.

As they stepped into the bowling alley, a man behind the shoe-rental counter looked up. When he recognized the Aldens, he smiled and waved. The children often bowled on the weekends with Grandfather.

"Hi, kids!" The man removed his wire-rimmed glasses. "I'll get shoes for you."

"Thanks anyway, Ron," Henry told the owner of the Greenfield Bowling Alley. "We're not here to bowl."

Benny stepped up to the counter. "We listen to the Big G!"

"What can I do for you then?" Ron asked, as if he hadn't even heard Benny's remark.

"Would you mind if we look around?" Jessie asked.

"Oh, I get it," Ron said, smiling. "You're taking part in that race, aren't you?"

Violet nodded. "The Great Detective Race."

"We listen to the Big G!" Benny repeated, a little louder this time.

Ron gave the youngest Alden a puzzled

look. "I heard you the first time, Benny," he said. Then he added, "Look around all you want."

It wasn't long before Benny was tugging on his brother's arm. "We're wasting our time here," he whispered.

Henry, who was checking out the bulletin board, looked over at her brother. "What makes you say that, Benny?" he wanted to know.

"I said the magic words twice and nothing happened."

Henry nodded. "I know, but I still think we're in the right place."

"I think so, too," said Jessie.

The Aldens went back to their search. But after a while, even Henry was having second thoughts.

"I haven't seen anything that looks like a clue," he told the others. "Have you?"

Jessie shook her head. "I don't get it," she said. "According to the riddle, it should be here."

"I guess we're on the wrong track again," Benny said sadly.

As they headed for the door, Ron called out, "Why not have a practice game while you're here. No charge."

Benny broke into a big grin. "Really?"

"Sure!" Ron set their bowling shoes on top of the counter. "The lanes are empty anyway."

"Thanks very much," said Jessie.

The children put all thoughts of the race aside for a while as they took turns rolling balls along the lane. When Benny knocked down all the pins, Henry, Jessie, and Violet cheered for him. They cheered even louder when he got a second strike, and then a third.

"Way to go, Benny!" said Jessie. "That's a record for you."

Just then, a turkey suddenly flashed on an overhead screen. They all burst out laughing.

"What's a—" Benny began to say, but Henry knew the question before his brother asked it.

"If you get three strikes in a row, it's called a turkey," he explained.

Jessie suddenly whirled around. A funny look came over her face. Then she clapped her hands and cried, "That's it!"

"What's it?" asked Violet.

"Remember the riddle?" Jessie said. *"Make your way to an alley,/ that's what you should do—"*

"Three strikes in a row/ and you'll find the next clue," finished Violet, who knew the words by heart.

"And I got three strikes in a row," said Benny, who still couldn't get over it.

"Yes, you did," Jessie said, giving her little brother a hug. "And we found the next clue!" She pointed to the turkey flashing on the screen.

"Our next clue is a turkey?" Benny echoed.

Violet giggled. "That's a strange clue."

"You can say that again!" Henry said. He was baffled. So were Violet and Benny.

But Jessie grinned. "I get it!" she said.

CHAPTER 5

Does Spelling Count?

"Where are we going, Jessie?" Benny wanted to know. He held the door open for the others as they stepped outside.

Jessie grinned. "There's a turkey wandering around Greenfield," she told him, "and it's time to track him down."

Violet's eyebrows shot up. "A turkey in Greenfield?"

"Not just an ordinary turkey," Jessie added mysteriously. "I'm talking about a giant turkey."

Henry gave Jessie a sideways glance. "A

giant turkey by the name of Dennis Howe, you mean?"

Jessie laughed. "Well, Dennis *is* dressed up like a turkey."

"A giant turkey!" cried Benny. He sounded excited.

"It's a long shot," Jessie admitted, "but we have to check out everything."

It took them a while, but the Aldens finally spotted Dennis in the town square. He was sitting on a bench beside the Minuteman statue.

Dennis waved as the children hurried over. "I had a hunch you'd be back," he said, fanning his face with a flyer.

"Guess what, Dennis?" said Benny. "We listen to the Big G!"

"Ah, the magic words!" Dennis chuckled as he reached into a feathered pocket. He tugged out an envelope and handed it to the youngest Alden.

Benny's face lit up. "We found the next clue!"

"Gobble, gobble," said Dennis.

"Thanks, Dennis," Henry said, laughing.

As they headed back across the brick pavement, Benny wasted no time opening the envelope. He pulled out a slip of paper and frowned.

"What is it, Benny?" Violet wanted to know.

Benny shrugged. "I've never seen a clue like this before."

Benny passed the note to Violet. Violet passed it to Henry. Then Henry passed it to Jessie. But nobody could make any sense of it.

"It's just some alphabet letters," said Violet. "H . . . I . . . J . . . K . . . L . . . M . . . N . . . O."

Jessie added, "And a picture of a slide."

"It's not much to go on." Benny crinkled his brow.

"What do you make of it, Henry?" Violet asked.

Henry thought for a second. "I'm not sure what the letters mean," he said, "but playgrounds have slides and swings."

"Hello again!" said a voice behind them.

They turned to see Amber Madison coming over.

"Oh, hello!" Jessie quickly shoved the clue into her pocket.

Amber laughed a little. "Our paths keep crossing, don't they? Bound to happen in a small town, I guess." Her gaze dropped to the envelope in Benny's hand. "Getting closer to the finish line?"

"The finish line?" Benny looked puzzled.

"I'm talking about the Great Detective Race," Amber explained. "I have a hunch you kids are ahead. Am I right?"

"Well, we *did* just find another clue," Benny said.

"No kidding!" Amber gave the Aldens a sharp look. "What kind of clue?"

Benny opened his mouth to answer, but Henry spoke first. "Actually, it doesn't make any sense to us yet," he said.

Jessie nodded. "It's a bit confusing."

"Well, let's see what you've got there." Amber held out a hand. "Maybe I can help."

Jessie caught Henry's eye. Why was Amber

so interested in the race, they wondered.

"Thanks, anyway," Violet said. "I know you mean well, but we have fun figuring things out on our own." She said this as nicely as she could.

Amber frowned. "I see," she said in an icy voice. "I have better things to do with my time anyway." The author's heels clicked along the brick pavement as she hurried away.

Henry let out a low whistle. "Wow," he said. "Amber Madison sure is interested in the Great Detective Race."

Jessie nodded. "It's funny how we keep running into her."

"Greenfield *is* a small town," Violet pointed out.

"That's true," Jessie agreed. Still, she couldn't help wondering if it wasn't more than just a coincidence. Was Amber following them?

*   *   *

The next morning, Jessie made a list of all the playgrounds in Greenfield. Then they set off to check every slide in town. When they finally stopped at a concession stand for lunch, Jessie pulled her notebook from her back pocket.

"Three more playgrounds to go," she said, glancing at their list, "and that's all."

"Don't worry," Benny said, as they made their way to an empty park bench. "We'll find the next clue."

"How can you be so sure, Benny?" asked Violet, sitting down beside Jessie.

"Because when you're looking for something," Benny explained, "it's always in the last place you look." He swallowed a bite of his hot dog.

Henry laughed. "That makes sense," he said. "When you find something, you don't bother looking anymore."

"What I can't figure out," Violet said, "is what the letters of the alphabet mean."

Jessie nodded. "I've been wondering about that, too."

"What were the letters again?" asked Benny, licking mustard from the corner of his mouth.

Violet answered, "H, I, J, K, L, M, N, O."

Jessie sipped her soda thoughtfully. "But why only H to O? That's the part I don't get."

"You got me," said Henry.

"Maybe there's another way of looking at it," Violet said.

The others looked at her. "Such as?"

"What if we switch the letters around?" Violet reasoned. "Maybe they'll spell out a message of some kind."

Henry thought about this. "Anything's possible."

The four Aldens put their heads together and came up with a list of words using the letters in the clue. After Jessie jotted them down in her notebook, she read them aloud:

MILK   OINK   KILN   OIL   HIM   LIMO

"It doesn't amount to much," Henry remarked.

Violet agreed. "I guess it was a bit of a leap."

Jessie looked at her watch. "Time's ticking away," she said, "and we still have three more playgrounds to check out."

After tossing their napkins and empty cups

into a trashcan, the children wheeled their bikes back onto the road and set off again.

They hadn't gone very far before Jessie slowed her bike to a stop.

Henry came up beside her. "What is it, Jessie?"

"I left my notebook on the park bench," Jessie said with a frown.

Circling back, the Aldens found the notebook right where Jessie had left it. Only, something wasn't quite right.

"A page is missing," Jessie pointed out. "See? Somebody tore out our list of playgrounds!"

They all looked at Jessie's notebook in astonishment. "I can't believe it!" said Henry.

"Who would do such a thing?" Violet wondered.

Benny had an answer. "Somebody looking for a clue," he said. "That's who."

The youngest Alden had a point. It had to be somebody who was tracking down the code word. And now that person knew as much as they did.

Henry gave Jessie a quick glance. Had she been right the other day? Was somebody really following them?

"Never mind," said Jessie. "I remember what was on the list. The next playground's in the Morningside neighborhood."

"Let's go," said Henry. "The race is on!"

When the Aldens arrived at the Morningside playground, they found children playing on the swings, on the monkey bars, and in the sandbox. But nobody was around the slide. They quickly checked it out, top to bottom. But they couldn't find anything unusual.

"Well, let's head for the next playground," Henry suggested, not wanting to waste any time.

But Benny saw something the others didn't. "What's that?"

The others looked in the direction he was pointing. A hopscotch game had been outlined in chalk on the pavement close by. A message was scrawled in one of the squares.

Taking a closer look, the children read what it said: *You will find something weerd at Potter's Creek.*

"Hooray!" Benny cheered. "We found the clue!"

"That's odd," Jessie said, as she jotted the message in her notebook. "The word 'weerd' is spelled wrong."

Benny frowned. "It is?"

"It should be w-e-i-r-d. Not w-e-e-r-d," Henry pointed out. "You're right, Jessie. That is kind of strange."

But Violet didn't think it was strange at all. "Debra said she wasn't a very good speller, remember?"

"It's too late to go all the way out to Potter's Creek today," Henry noted, glancing at his watch.

Jessie nodded. "It'll take at least an hour to get there. Let's wait until the morning."

"Hey!" Something caught Henry's eye.

"Isn't that the boy from the mall?"

The others looked over. A boy wearing baggy pants and a red T-shirt was zooming away on a skateboard.

"Yes, I'm sure of it," said Jessie. "He was signing up for the Great Detective Race."

Benny nodded. "He's even wearing a WGFD baseball cap."

Jessie and Henry exchanged puzzled glances. How odd that the boy was at the park the same time they were. Was he following the list of playgrounds torn from Jessie's notebook?

CHAPTER 6

A Big Question Mark

"Let's pack a lunch and take it to Potter's Creek with us," Violet suggested the next morning.

"That's an awesome idea!" cried Benny. He got out the peanut butter and jelly.

Jessie reached the thermos down from the cupboard. "It's a beautiful day for a picnic in the country."

"Let's pack lots of sandwiches," Benny suggested. "Detective work always makes me hungry."

This made Henry laugh. "Everything makes you hungry, Benny!" He put a loaf of bread, some cold cuts, lettuce, and mustard on the counter.

"We're supposed to find something weird at Potter's Creek," Violet said, as she washed the lettuce. "I wonder what we'll find."

Henry shrugged. "Could be anything."

"It's strange how we figured out the last clue," Violet added.

"What do you mean, Violet?" Jessie wondered.

"Well, we never did make sense of those alphabet letters."

"Now that you mention it, Violet," said Henry, "I guess we didn't." He took some apples from the refrigerator.

"We found the hopscotch clue without them," Benny said proudly. "And that means we're very good detectives."

Violet frowned. She wasn't so sure that's what it meant. She didn't like leaving any loose ends.

After cleaning up the kitchen, the children loaded their picnic lunch into Jessie's backpack and set off for Potter's Creek on their bicycles.

"I'm glad I brought my camera," Violet said as she rode along. "It's so beautiful out here in the country." Photography was one of Violet's hobbies. She often took her camera along when the Aldens went on trips.

Jessie nodded. "I love the smell of the wildflowers."

Benny, who was riding in front with Henry, suddenly called back, "There's Potter's Creek!"

Sure enough, they soon came to a creek winding its way across a clover meadow and under a narrow bridge. Henry propped his bike against a tree. So did the others.

Benny glanced all around. "I think Amber was right," he said with a grin.

"About what?" Jessie asked him.

"About us leading the pack," said Benny. "I don't see anybody else looking for clues."

"That's true." Jessie looked off into the distance. "We seem to be the only ones here."

"So where do we start?" Violet asked, as

they scrambled down to the creek.

"Let's split up," Jessie suggested in her practical way. "We can cover more ground that way."

"Good idea," said Henry. "If anybody sees anything, shout."

Jessie and Benny checked along one side of the creek. Henry and Violet searched along the other. When they reached the woods, Jessie noticed Benny eyeing her backpack. She guessed what was coming next.

"You want something to eat," she said. "Right, Benny?"

"Well, I am kind of hungry," Benny said with a nod. Then he called out, "Anybody else ready to eat?"

"Count me in," Henry shouted, giving his little brother the thumbs-up sign.

Violet snapped a few photos as they made themselves comfortable on the grassy bank. Jessie handed out the sandwiches while Henry opened the thermos.

"Uh-oh," said Benny. "I think somebody's watching us." He was holding out his special cup as Henry poured the lemonade. It was the cracked pink cup he had found when they were living in the boxcar.

Benny was right. Somebody was standing on the bridge in the distance—watching them through binoculars! Then, as if realizing the Aldens were looking that way, the figure suddenly hurried away.

"I wonder who that was," said Violet.

"I bet it was somebody else looking for a clue," Henry said, as he unwrapped a ham sandwich.

"I'm sure you're right, Henry," said Jessie. She wasn't really sure, but she didn't want to alarm the younger children. She still couldn't shake the feeling they were being followed.

"I guess we're not ahead after all," said Benny. He didn't sound very happy.

"We still have the other side of the bridge to check out," Violet said, trying to sound positive. "I have a feeling we'll find a clue before too long."

"Maybe," Henry said. "But we might be on a wild-goose chase."

Jessie agreed. "I'm been thinking the same thing, Henry."

Violet had to admit it was possible. "This is a funny place to hide a clue," she said. "In the middle of nowhere."

"It's not just that," said Henry. "Potter's Creek is outside of town." He paused for a moment to let them think about it. "Debra Belmont said all the clues were hidden around Greenfield."

"But the riddle said we'd find something weird at Potter's Creek," Benny reminded them.

Jessie frowned. "I have a hunch somebody planted a fake clue."

"And we fell for it," added Henry. "That's the kicker."

"You mean, somebody played a trick on us?" A frown crossed Benny's round face as the idea began to sink in. "But . . . why?"

Jessie had an opinion about this. "To throw us off the track."

"I guess somebody was afraid we'd beat them to the code word," Henry concluded.

"Who would do something like that?" Benny wondered.

"You know," said Violet, "I keep thinking about that boy on the skateboard."

Jessie nodded. "It does seem like an awfully strange coincidence that he was at the Morningside playground."

"Maybe he was tracking down clues," Benny suggested. "Just like us."

"I wish I could believe that," Violet said. "But I don't."

"Neither do I," said Henry. "I have a hunch he was the one who tore the page from Jessie's notebook."

"If he did," Violet reasoned, "then he knew we were headed for the Morningside playground."

Jessie bit her lip. "And when we went back to get my notebook—" she began.

"He had time to get to the playground and plant the fake clue," finished Henry.

Jessie nodded as she poured lemonade into her cup. "Remember what he said when he was signing up for the race?"

"'Does spelling count?'" Henry replied. "Those were his exact words."

"That would explain the spelling mistake in the message," said Jessie.

"That's true," said Henry. "But we shouldn't jump to any conclusions until we have more evidence."

Jessie had another thought. "The boy on the skateboard isn't the only suspect."

The others turned to her, puzzled.

"I think we should include Amber Madison on our list."

Benny looked confused. "But Jessie, Amber isn't even in the race."

"That's right," Violet said with a nod. "She's only in town to promote her book."

"But she wants an radio interview so she can promote it," Jessie pointed out. "She wasn't very happy to be stuck on the Late Night show—but Mike Devlin will be interviewing the winner of the race on his daytime show."

"So, if Amber wins," said Violet, "she'll get an interview with Mike. Is that what you're saying, Jessie?"

"That's exactly what I'm saying."

"You might be on to something, Jessie," Henry said thoughtfully. "She could've heard us telling Debra about all the mysteries we've solved."

"That would explain why she keeps pumping us for information," Violet realized.

Benny crunched into an apple. "You think Amber planted the fake clue?"

"I wouldn't be surprised." Jessie tossed the sandwich wrappers into her backpack. "I bet she was afraid we were close to finding the code word."

Henry had something to add. "There's one other person we should add to our list of suspects—Debra Belmont."

"Debra Belmont?" said Jessie.

"You think Debra sent us on a wild-goose chase, Henry?" asked Violet.

"I don't want to think she'd do something like that, Violet," he told her. "But we have to consider everyone. And Mike Devlin told her to make sure a kid doesn't win the race."

Benny frowned. "But Debra was so nice to us."

"I hear you, Benny," said Henry. "But I don't think we can rule her out as a suspect."

"What are we going to do now?" Benny asked.

"I know what we're not going to do," said Henry. "We're not going to give up."

"No, we're not," Jessie agreed. "And if the hopscotch clue was a fake, then we're back to figuring out what the alphabet letters mean."

Benny scratched his head. "I'm not sure I remember the letters," he said. "Oh, yes, I do!" He began to tick each one off on his fingers. "H, I, J, K, L, M, N, O."

"What could it mean?" Jessie wondered.

Nobody had an answer.

CHAPTER 7

Through the Looking Glass

"Ice cream would sure hit the spot right now!" Benny called out, as the Aldens wheeled back into Greenfield.

"Sounds good to me," Henry was quick to agree. Jessie and Violet nodded.

When they stopped outside the Greenfield Ice-Cream Parlor, Violet decided to take another picture. Henry, Jessie, and Benny smiled into the camera while she snapped a photo, then they went inside.

"This was a great idea, Benny," Jessie said,

as they claimed an empty table by the window.

It only took them a few minutes to decide on what they wanted. Their order included a hot-fudge sundae for Henry, a waffle cone with two scoops of chocolate-mint ice cream for Jessie, a strawberry milkshake for Violet, and a banana split for Benny.

"And four glasses of water, please," Jessie added.

"Four glasses of H_2O coming right up!" The waitress gave them a cheery smile, then hurried away.

Jessie stared after her in amazement. Then she turned to the others, her eyes wide. "Did you hear that?"

Benny crinkled his brow. "What's H_2O?"

"That's what scientists call water," Henry explained, in an excited whisper.

"Oh," said Benny, still not sure what all the fuss was about.

Jessie smiled over at her little brother and sister. "What were the letters in the clue?"

"H, I, J, K, L, M, N, O," said Violet. Then

she suddenly gasped. "H to O!"

Henry grinned. "I think we just found the missing piece of the puzzle."

"I don't get it," said Benny, pulling a leaf from his hair.

"The puzzle showed the letters H to O," Jessie explained. "And H_2O is another name for water."

"And if we put 'water' and 'slide' together," put in Henry, "we get—"

"Waterslide!" the others cried out in unison.

Jessie nodded. "Maybe the clue's pointing us to the Greenfield Waterslides."

"That's a fun place to look for a clue!" Benny exclaimed after gulping down his water.

"So was the bowling alley," agreed Violet.

"And the ice cream truck," said Jessie. "Debra said she wanted the race to appeal to kids."

"Well, it does," said Benny. "Right, Henry?"

Before Henry had a chance to speak, a familiar voice caught their attention. They looked over to see Debra Belmont sitting at a table nearby. She was sipping an ice-cream soda through a straw and talking on a cell phone.

"I'm telling you, I have no choice but to fix it," Debra was saying into the phone. "What else can I do?"

Violet frowned. "I wonder why she sounds so upset?"

"I know, I know!" Debra was nodding her head. "If there's a leak, I'll have to walk."

Jessie's gaze jumped to Henry's. Neither of them liked what they were hearing.

Just then, Debra pocketed her cell phone, pushed back her chair, and walked out of the ice-cream parlor.

"That was odd," Henry said, as the door closed behind her. "I wonder if Debra was talking about the race."

"It sure sounded like it," said Jessie. "Do you think she's planning to fix it?"

"Fix the race?" Benny scrunched up his face. "Is it broken?"

"Fixing a race means something else, Benny," Henry said. "It means making sure a certain person wins."

"In this case, somebody between the ages of twenty and fifty," Jessie added. "The age of Mike Devlin's radio listeners."

"But what did she mean about a leak?" Benny wondered.

"I'm not sure," said Jessie. "I guess if word leaks out about the race being fixed, Debra would be forced to walk out on her job."

"Oh, Jessie!" cried Violet. "You don't really think she'd fix the race, do you?"

"It does sound suspicious, Violet," said Jessie.

But Violet wasn't convinced. "We can't be sure that Debra was talking about the race." Violet didn't like to think Debra would do something so dishonest.

"I suppose you're right," Jessie said, backing down a little. Violet had a point. It was one thing to suspect somebody. It was another thing to have proof.

As their ice cream arrived, the Aldens ate in silence. They were each thinking the same thing. Nothing was going to stop them from winning the Great Detective Race!

*   *   *

"Did you see how fast I went down that last one?" Benny asked the next afternoon.

The Aldens were sitting on the edge of the pool, taking a breather from the waterslides.

Jessie grinned. "I think you broke all the records, Benny," she said, as she rubbed sunscreen on her shoulders.

Violet looked over at her little brother. "I got a good shot of you coming down, Benny."

Benny beamed. "Cool!"

"I wonder where the next clue could be," Henry said thoughtfully. He was craning his neck as he glanced around.

Jessie slapped a hand against her forehead. "I almost forgot why we came."

Benny noticed a lifeguard wearing a WGFD baseball cap standing nearby. On the spur of the moment, he cupped his hands around his mouth and called out, "We listen to the Big G!"

The lifeguard jerked his head around in surprise. He was all smiles as he walked over. "Are you sure about that, young man?" he asked, a twinkle in his eye.

Benny paused. "We do listen to it sometimes," he replied. "But just not all the time."

The lifeguard laughed. "At least you're honest." He reached into the backpack slung over his shoulder and pulled out an envelope. "I haven't given away too many of these yet." He held the envelope out to Benny. "Good luck!"

"Wow!" Henry shook his head in disbelief. "How easy was that?"

"It was a nice change, that's for sure," said Jessie, as Benny pulled the next clue from the envelope.

Violet unfolded the sheet of paper Benny handed her. Then she read the words aloud:

Through a looking glass
all will be shown;
the code word you're seeking
is made out of stone.

"It's the last clue!" Jessie said.

"Got to be," said Henry. "It leads to the code word."

Violet couldn't help noticing that her little brother was unusually quiet. She could tell something was troubling him. "Is anything wrong, Benny?"

"The lifeguard said he gave away some of these clues already," Benny answered. "Somebody might beat us to the code word."

"The lifeguard said he hasn't given away too many," Henry said. "We still have a chance."

At that, Jessie read the riddle aloud a second time. After some thought, she said, "If the answer is made out of stone, maybe we should be looking for a statue."

Henry nodded. "That makes sense."

"Wait!" Violet snapped her fingers. "How about the Minuteman statue in the town square?"

"That's a good guess, Violet," Henry told her. "But the Minuteman statue is bronze—not stone."

"You're right, Henry." Violet nodded. "I forgot about that."

"What does it mean about a looking glass?" Benny wondered.

"A looking glass is an old-fashioned word for a mirror," Jessie told him.

"Oh, I get it," said Benny. "Because you look at yourself in it, right?"

"You catch on fast," said Henry.

"I read a book about a girl who steps through a looking glass," Violet said thoughtfully. "She suddenly finds herself in a different world."

Jessie nodded. *"Alice Through the Looking Glass,"* she recalled. "It's about the same girl from *Alice in Wonderland.*"

Nobody said anything for a while. They were each lost in thought about the riddle.

CHAPTER 8

Mirror, Mirror, on the Wall

"I was just wondering," Violet said at breakfast the next morning, "do you think we should check out the House of Mirrors?"

"That store in the mall?" Henry paused as he cut his pancake with the side of his fork. "Seems a bit far-fetched, don't you think?"

"It might be worth a shot," Jessie said. She passed the platter of bacon to Henry. "Don't you think?"

"I suppose you're right." Henry nodded. "The riddle *did* mention a looking glass."

Benny nodded as he polished off his orange juice. "And that's a kind of mirror."

"Right, but . . . don't forget the last part of the riddle," Henry reminded them. "The code word is made out of stone."

The Aldens left the kitchen spic-and-span, then headed for the mall. After dropping Violet's film off at the one-hour photo shop, they made their way to the House of Mirrors.

Each mirror was different from the next. Some were tinted, some were plain. Some were star-shaped, some were half-moons. Some were full-length, some hung from chains. The four children peered long and hard at each and every one. But after trying the magic words on the salesclerk, they finally turned to each other in dismay.

"That didn't exactly pan out, did it?" Violet said, as they left the store.

"Never mind," said Henry. "We have to consider every possibility."

As they walked through the mall, Benny began to recite the riddle aloud in a sing-songy voice. *"Through a looking glass/all will be shown;/ the code word you're seeking/ is made out of stone."*

"I'm not sure what to make of it," Jessie said. "Any ideas, Henry?"

But Henry wasn't listening. He was looking over at a man in a business suit who was sitting on a bench. "Isn't that Chopper Dan?" he asked.

The others followed their brother's gaze. A tall man with curly hair was talking to a boy about Henry's age. The boy had a WGFD baseball cap on backwards—and he didn't look very happy.

Jessie nodded. "I think you're right, Henry." She recognized the curly-haired man from the WGFD posters.

Benny's eyes widened. "And that's the boy who signed up for the race," he realized. "The one on the skateboard."

Just then, Chopper Dan got to his feet and walked away. When he was gone, the boy slouched down on the bench, his arms folded.

"I wonder what that was about," said Violet.

Henry shrugged. "There's no way of knowing."

As if feeling their eyes on him, the boy suddenly looked over. When Benny waved, the boy waved back.

"Come on," said Jessie. "Let's go over and say hello."

As the Aldens headed his way, the boy sat up a bit straighter.

"Hi!" Henry greeted him with a friendly smile. "You signed up for the race, right?" The boy nodded. "We signed up for it, too. I'm Henry. And these are my sisters, Jessie and Violet. And that's my brother, Benny."

"I'm Chris Beamer." The boy shook hands with Henry. Then he shook hands with everyone else.

"Are you having any luck?" Violet asked him shyly. "With the race, I mean."

"Not really," he said with a shrug. "How about you?"

"Well, it's not easy," Jessie replied. "But we're hanging in."

Chris heaved a sigh. "Well, at least *somebody* still has a chance for a helicopter ride."

There was something in the way Chris

said *somebody* that alerted Jessie. "But you still have a chance, too," she said. "Right?"

"Not anymore."

Benny's face fell. "You mean—somebody won?"

"What?" Chris looked over at Benny. "No, what I meant was, I'm out."

The Aldens looked at each other in surprise. "You gave up?" Benny asked him.

"Not exactly," said Chris. "I just found out I'm not allowed to be in the race."

"Oh, kids are allowed to enter the race," Jessie argued. "I'm sure of it."

Chris shook his head. "Not if somebody in the family works at the station," he pointed out. "Somebody like Chopper Dan."

"Somebody like Chopper Dan?" Benny repeated, not understanding.

"Don't you get it?" said Chris. "I'm Dan Beamer's son."

"Chopper Dan"—Benny paused—"is your father?"

"Yup," Chris answered with a frown. "I signed up so I could get a ride in the WGFD helicopter. But my dad just told me it was against the rules. For family members to enter the race, I mean."

"That's too bad," Violet said in her soft voice. "But I'm sure your dad will take you for a ride another time."

"He's not allowed to take anyone up with him," Chris informed them. "The only person who can ride with him is the winner of the race."

"Wow," said Henry. "That's a tough break."

Chris shrugged, then got up and walked away.

"Poor Chris!" said Violet. "I wish we could do something."

"Me, too," Henry said. "But I'm afraid we can't change the radio station's rules."

After picking up Violet's snapshots, the children were on their way out of the mall when they almost bumped into Debra Belmont. The young woman was carrying a large cardboard box.

"Hi, kids!" she said, laughing a little. "I should watch where I'm going."

"Do you need some help with that?" Henry asked, nodding towards the box.

"Are you sure you don't mind?" Debra looked surprised—and pleased. "It isn't very heavy, but it is rather awkward."

Henry didn't mind at all. "Are you on your way to the WGFD booth?" he asked, taking the box from her.

Debra nodded. "We ran out of ball caps," she explained as they headed back through the mall. "I had to dash over to the station to get some more. It's a long walk."

Jessie gave her a questioning look. "You walked all the way across town?"

"Yes, my car's at the garage," Debra explained. "It was leaking oil, so I had to get it fixed."

The Aldens exchanged glances. That must've been the phone conversation they'd over-heard. Debra had been talking about fixing her car—not the race! Violet smiled a little. She knew Debra could never do anything dishonest.

After helping Debra with the box, the Aldens found an empty bench by the fountain. They sat down to look through Violet's photos.

There was one of Jessie picking wildflowers that was off-center. And another one of Henry on his bike that was a bit blurry. But most of the snapshots had turned out great.

"I really like this one," Violet said.

"Which one is that?" asked Jessie, looking over.

"The one of Benny coming down the waterslide," replied Violet, passing the photo to her sister.

"How about this one?" Jessie held up the snapshot taken in front of the ice-cream parlor. "You're becoming a wonderful photographer, Violet." She passed the photo to Henry.

"Thanks, Jessie," Violet said gratefully. "But I still have a lot to learn," she added modestly.

"That's funny," Henry said, almost to himself. He stared at the snapshot.

"What is it?" Jessie asked, looking over at her brother.

"Take a look at the two people across from the ice-cream parlor." Henry passed the snapshot back to Jessie.

Jessie looked from the photo to Henry and back again. "Is that Mike Devlin?"

"Mike Devlin *and* Amber Madison," said Violet, who was peering over Jessie's shoulder.

"I wonder what they're talking about," said Jessie.

"Maybe Mike decided to interview her after all," guessed Benny.

"Maybe," said Jessie. But something didn't feel right.

"Remember what you said, Jessie?" Violet pointed out, as she tucked the photos back into the envelope. "One mystery at a time."

Jessie laughed. "You're right, Violet," she said. "We have a code word to find."

As the children got up to leave, Benny fished a penny out of his pocket. He tossed it into the fountain.

"Did you make a wish, Benny?" Henry asked, coming up behind him.

Benny nodded. "I wished we could find—" The youngest Alden suddenly stopped talking.

"What is it, Benny?" Jessie could tell by her little brother's face that something was up.

Benny pointed. "Look!"

CHAPTER 9

Crossing the Finish Line

Benny was pointing to the mermaid in the fountain. "Alice is holding a mirror!"

Violet caught her breath. "And she's made out of stone!"

"That's it!" Benny almost shouted. "The code word is 'Alice.'"

"You're a genius!" Jessie said proudly.

"I guess I *am* kind of smart for my age," Benny had to admit.

"You're smart for *any* age, Benny!" Violet gave her little brother a warm hug.

Henry added, "Now there's only one thing left to do."

"What's that, Henry?" Jessie wondered.

"Cross the finish line!" Henry jerked his head in the direction of the WGFD booth.

The others looked over to where Mike Devlin was sitting behind the microphone. The deejay was snapping his fingers in time to the music.

"Come on!" cried Benny, who was already racing for the booth.

But somebody else was headed in that direction, too. It was Amber Madison—and she reached the finish line just seconds before the Aldens.

Debra, who was unpacking ball caps, looked up. "Oh, you're back again, Miss Madison?" she said with a frown. "If this is about switching your interview to the daytime . . . "

"It's not," Amber replied, cutting her short. "I'm here about the Great Detective Race."

"Oh?" Debra seemed surprised to hear this.

"I found the code word!" declared Amber.

The Aldens could hardly believe their ears.

Were they too late to win the race?

Just then, Mike Devlin gestured for Amber to join him. As the author stepped into the WGFD booth, Mike spoke into the microphone.

"Well, folks!" he announced. "Somebody just stopped by our booth. Looks like we just might have a winner in the Great Detective Race." Turning to Amber, he added, "How about telling our listeners a bit about yourself. Do you live here in Greenfield?"

"No, I'm an author from out of town. My name's Amber Madison," she said, "and my book—which is on sale now—is called *The Art of Good Manners.*"

"Well, nice to meet you, Amber," Mike said in his smooth voice. "So you think you've tracked down the code word, do you?"

Benny held his breath. He couldn't stand the suspense.

"No doubt about it!" Amber sounded very sure. "The code word is . . . 'mermaid!'"

"Yes, you hit the nail right on the—*what?*" Mike did a double take. "What did you say?"

Amber leaned closer to the microphone. "'Mermaid,'" she repeated. "Now, about my book—"

"Um, no . . . I'm afraid that isn't the code word," Mike said, shaking his head in confusion.

For a long moment, Amber stared at Mike. Finally she said, "What . . . what do you mean?" She sounded puzzled. "Of course that's it!"

Mike held up a hand. "Time for some mellow tunes from Lark Sanders," he said, speaking into the microphone. As music boomed from the overhead speakers, he quickly hustled the author from the booth.

"That was pretty strange, wasn't it?" Jessie said, keeping her voice low. "Mike seemed to be expecting a different answer."

Henry nodded.

Amber whirled around to face the deejay. "What's going on?" she demanded angrily. "I gave you the right code word—and you know it!"

"Please," Mike told her, "try to calm down."

"I will *not* calm down!" Amber was talking

loudly now. "Not until you tell me what this is all about!" She folded her arms in front of her.

As shoppers gathered round, Mike ran his fingers nervously through his neatly combed hair. "This isn't the time or the place—" he began.

"I won't be cheated out of a win!" Amber broke in. "I guessed the correct code word. End of story."

The Aldens looked at each other. They knew this was the moment to speak up.

"Actually," said Henry, "we think the code word is 'Alice.'"

Debra began to clap her hands. "Yes, yes, that's it!" Turning to Mike, she added, "Looks like we have a winner after all."

As a murmur went up from the crowd, Amber glared over at the Aldens. "And who on earth is Alice?" she wanted to know.

"It's a nickname for the mermaid," Jessie explained. "Everyone in Greenfield calls her Alice."

"You were *this* close, Miss Madison." Debra

pinched her thumb and finger together. "But it was the *name* of the mermaid we were after."

"Listen, Debra," Mike said, "we can't really expect someone from Boston to know what folks around here call the mermaid. Can we?" He lifted a shoulder in a shrug. "I say she was close enough. Let's just declare Amber the winner."

"We can't do that, Mike," Debra said firmly. "It wouldn't be fair to the Aldens—or to anyone else in the race."

Before the deejay could answer, Henry spoke up. "How did you know Amber Madison was from Boston?" he wondered.

It was a good question. Amber had said she was from out of town, but nothing else. How could Mike know? Everyone waited for an answer.

The question seemed to catch Mike off guard. "I, um . . . had a hunch, that's all. What's the big deal?"

Debra looked over at the deejay suspiciously, but she didn't say anything.

"Maybe Amber mentioned it yesterday," Jessie hinted.

"What are you driving at?" Mike asked. "I never met this lady before today."

"Are you sure about that?" Violet questioned. Then she turned to Debra. "I have something you should see." After shuffling through her snapshots, Violet handed Debra the photo taken outside the ice-cream parlor.

"No wonder you knew Amber was from Boston," Debra realized. She was staring at the photograph with a frown.

"What are you talking about?" Mike shifted uncomfortably.

"How would you explain this, Mike?" Debra passed the snapshot to him. "It clearly shows that you and Amber Madison *have* met before."

Amber inched her way closer to look over Mike's shoulder. As she got a glimpse of the photograph, her mouth dropped.

"You fixed the race, didn't you, Mike?" Debra said accusingly. "You told Amber that the mermaid was the code word."

Mike was at a loss for words. He looked over at Amber.

"Are you waiting for *me* to say something, Mike?" the author asked him in disbelief. "Fixing the race was your idea, not mine." She threw up her hands. "I should've known better than to trust some small-town dee-jay."

"Now wait just a minute…" Mike began.

"No, you wait!" Amber snapped. "You told me the mermaid was the code word. How should I know anything about her nickname?" Her dark eyes flashed angrily. "I should have stuck with the Aldens."

Jessie and Henry exchanged glances. "You were at Potter's Creek, weren't you?" Jessie guessed.

"You were watching us through binoculars," added Violet.

Debra gave the author a sideways glance. "You were actually spying on these children, Miss Madison?"

Amber didn't deny it. "I heard them talking

at the mall about being good detectives. I asked around and somebody told me they were the Aldens. I was hoping they'd lead me to the code word."

"But . . . why?" Debra was shaking her head in disbelief.

"You wanted an interview on Mike Devlin's show," Henry said. "Right?"

"Yes," admitted Amber, surprised that Henry knew that. "Mike was interviewing the winner of the race, so . . . I signed up."

"And you left a fake clue!" Benny accused her. "That wasn't very nice."

"Fake clue?" Amber looked surprised. "I *did* get carried away," she admitted. "I should never have followed you around town. But I had nothing to do with any fake clue."

The children looked at each other. They had a feeling Amber was telling the truth.

"Well, no harm done, right?" Mike put in, trying to make light of everything. Then he turned to Amber with a shrug. "An interview on our Late Night show isn't as bad as all that. Is it?"

"You must be kidding!" Amber snorted. "I want nothing more to do with this second-rate station. You won't be seeing me around here again," she said, walking away. "Not ever!"

"We're counting on it," Debra called after her.

CHAPTER 10

Swan Cake

"Look," said Benny. "It's Mr. Porter!"

Sure enough, the owner of the radio station stepped out from amongst the shoppers. "What's going on?" he asked.

"Oh, nothing really," Mike was quick to say. "We were just congratulating the winners of the Great Detective Race." With a sweep of his arm, he pointed towards the children. "The Aldens!"

"Well, how about that!" Mr. Porter gave them a big smile. "When I saw the crowd, I thought something might be wrong."

"Now, what could be wrong?" asked Mike.

"Actually," said Debra, "there *is* a problem, Mr. Porter."

The station owner's face grew stern as Debra told him about Amber Madison. He frowned as he looked at the photo. "How could you do something so dishonest, Mike?" he wanted to know.

"Hey, I just didn't want kids to win the race," Mike said with a shrug. "I did what was best for the station, that's all."

"For the station," Mr. Porter asked, "or for you?"

"What's the difference?" Mike snapped. "I'm the reason for the Big G's success. Everybody knows that."

"Mike, I've always said it takes teamwork to make a station successful," Mr. Porter said quietly. "But I don't think you're a team player."

"I can see why you're upset, but—"

"Here's the deal, Mike," Mr. Porter interrupted. "Everybody deserves a second chance, so I'm not going to fire you. You will, however, be working the Late Night show for a while."

Mike's jaw dropped. "You can't be serious!"

"I run an honest station, Mike," the station owner replied. "We're planning more contests during the daytime and I just can't trust you."

"Look, I'm sorry I betrayed your trust, Mr. Porter." Mike shifted uncomfortably. "I should never have done that, but . . . can't we sit down and talk about this?"

Mr. Porter shook his head. "My decision is final, Mike. You won't be back on the daytime show until you prove you're a team player."

Mike opened his mouth, then closed it again. Finally, he walked back to the WGFD booth, looking truly sorry.

"Congratulations," Debra said, turning to the Aldens. She held out two envelopes. "Here's your tickets to *Swan Lake*—and a voucher for a ride in the sky with Chopper Dan."

"Thanks!" said Benny.

"But there's only room in the helicopter for one other person," Debra added. "I suppose you'll have to draw straws."

"Or put your names into a hat," said a voice behind them.

The Aldens turned to see Chris standing with his father, Chopper Dan. Chris was giving the Aldens the thumbs-up sign.

Henry, Jessie, Violet, and Benny looked at each other. "Are you thinking what I'm thinking?" Violet asked her sister and brothers.

Jessie nodded. So did Benny and Henry.

Benny held the envelope out to Chris. "You take it," he said. "Now you can get a ride with your dad."

Chris stared at the envelope. "What . . . ?"

Henry said, "We want you to have it."

Chris hesitated. "But . . . I haven't been very nice."

"You left that clue in the hopscotch game," guessed Jessie. "Didn't you?"

Chris nodded. "I heard you talking about all the mysteries you've solved," he confessed. "I didn't think I had a chance to win."

Benny blinked in surprise. "You sent us on a wild-goose chase?"

"Yes," he said. "I saw you in the park the other day. When you left your notebook on the bench . . . "

"You tore out the list of playgrounds, didn't you?" guessed Violet. "Then you planted that fake clue in the hopscotch game."

Chris didn't deny it.

Chopper Dan looked at his son in disbelief. "Why would you do such a thing, Chris?"

"I wanted to throw the Aldens off track." Chris hung his head. "Getting a ride in the helicopter was so important to me. I figured the race was just a game to them."

"It wasn't just a game to us," Violet exclaimed.

"It was more than that," agreed Jessie. "A lot more."

Henry added, "We were trying to win tickets to *Swan Lake* for our housekeeper, Mrs. McGregor."

"I'm really sorry," Chris said, handing the envelope back to Henry. "I don't deserve this."

Chopper Dan shook his head in surprise.

"You wanted a helicopter ride that much?" he asked his son. "I had no idea."

"I think we can work something out," said Mr. Porter. "We'll make sure you get that ride in the sky with your dad, Chris."

"Thanks so much!" said Chris. Then, turning to the Aldens, he added, "Sorry about the fake clue."

"If you mean that," said Jessie, "then you won't play tricks on people anymore."

"I won't," Chris promised. "Not ever."

*　　*　　*

The next day, Henry, Jessie, Violet, and Benny trooped into the dining room where Grandfather and Mrs. McGregor were waiting. Henry was carrying a birthday cake while everyone sang "Happy Birthday" at the top of their lungs. Even Watch woof-woof-woofed his way through the song.

"Oh, how beautiful!" Mrs. McGregor said, as Henry set the cake on the table.

"It's your favorite," Jessie told her. "Chocolate with caramel frosting."

"Well, fancy that," said Mrs. McGregor. "And just look at those sprinkles on the top—in the shape of a swan!"

"Well, you couldn't get tickets to *Swan Lake*," Henry said, his eyes twinkling, "so we made you a swan cake."

"How thoughtful!" said Mrs. McGregor.

"Now make a wish, Mrs. McGregor," Benny said. "Sometimes wishes really do come true."

Their housekeeper closed her eyes, took a deep breath, and blew out all the candles.

"Well done!" said Grandfather, as everyone clapped.

Benny held out an envelope. "Open this first, Mrs. McGregor," he said. "Okay?"

Mrs. McGregor smiled at the youngest Alden. Then she opened the envelope Benny handed her. "Why, it's a sketch of Watch!" she said, as she pulled out a birthday card.

"Violet drew it herself," Benny said proudly.

"But everybody helped with the verse inside," Violet was quick to add.

Mrs. McGregor opened the card and read the verse aloud.

We entered a race
and followed the clues
so somebody's wishes
all would come true!

"Happy birthday, Mrs. McGregor!" Jessie handed their housekeeper another envelope.

"Oh, my!" said Mrs. McGregor. "What's this?"

"Open it, Mrs. McGregor!" cried Benny. He was bouncing up and down with excitement.

The Aldens held their breath as she opened the envelope.

"Front-row tickets to *Swan Lake?*" the housekeeper blinked in surprise. "How in the world . . . ?"

"It wasn't easy, Mrs. McGregor," Henry said with a grin. "First, we followed the Pied Piper, then—"

"We tracked down a giant turkey!" continued Benny.

"And don't forget about the mermaid," added Violet.

Mrs. McGregor laughed. "You know what?" she said. "I can't wait to hear all about it!"

GERTRUDE CHANDLER WARNER discovered when she was teaching that many readers who like an exciting story could find no books that were both easy and fun to read. She decided to try to meet this need, and her first book, The Boxcar Children, quickly proved she had succeeded.

Miss Warner drew on her own experiences to write the mystery. As a child she spent hours watching trains go by on the tracks opposite her family home. She often dreamed about what it would be like to set up housekeeping in a caboose or freight car—the situation the Alden children find themselves in.

While the mystery element is central to each of Miss Warner's books, she never thought of them as strictly juvenile mysteries. She liked to stress the Aldens' independence and resourcefulness and their solid New England devotion to using up and making do. The Aldens go about most of their adventures with as little adult supervision as possible—something else that delights young readers.

Miss Warner lived in Putnam, Connecticut, until her death in 1979. During her lifetime, she received hundreds of letters from girls and boys telling her how much they liked her books.